KT-423-603

JILL MURPHY

THE WORST WITCH

PUFFIN BOOKS

PUFFIN BOOKS

Published by the Penguin Group
Penguin Books Ltd, 27 Wrights Lane, London W8 5TZ, England
Penguin Putnam Inc., 375 Hudson Street, New York, New York 10014, USA
Penguin Books Australia Ltd, Ringwood, Victoria, Australia
Penguin Books Canada Ltd, 10 Alcorn Avenue, Toronto, Ontario, Canada M4V 3B2
Penguin Books (NZ) Ltd, Private Bag 102902, NSMC, Auckland, New Zealand

Penguin Books Ltd, Registered Offices: Harmondsworth, Middlesex, England

First published by Allison & Busby 1974
Published in Puffin Books 1978
Published in Young Puffin Modern Classics 1996
Published in this edition 1998
1 3 5 7 9 10 8 6 4 2

Copyright © Jill Murphy, 1974
Afterword copyright © Stephanie Nettell, 1996
All rights reserved

Set in Bembo

Made and printed in England by Clays Ltd, St Ives plc

ISBN 0–141–30370–0

The Worst Witch

Jill Murphy was born in London in 1949. From a very early age she was drawing and writing stories, and was already putting books together (literally, with a stapler) by the time she was six. She went on to study at Chelsea, Croydon and Camberwell Schools of Art. Jill worked in a children's home for four years and as a nanny for a year, before becoming a freelance writer and illustrator. The Worst Witch stories, of which this is the first, are some of Puffin's most outstandingly successful titles. Jill lives in London with her son, Charlie.

Once you have finished reading *The Worst Witch* you may be interested in reading the Afterword by Stephanie Nettell on page 96.

For Reeeney

 ISS Cackle's Academy for Witches stood at the top of a high mountain surrounded by a pine forest. It looked more like a prison than a school, with its gloomy grey walls and

turrets. Sometimes you could see the pupils on their broomsticks flitting like bats above the playground wall, but usually the place was half hidden in mist, so that if you had glanced up at the mountain you would probably not have noticed the building was there at all.

Everything about the school was dark and shadowy. There were long, narrow corridors and winding staircases – and of course there were the girls themselves, dressed in black gymslips, black stockings, black hob-nailed boots, grey shirts and black-and-grey ties. Even their summer dresses were black-and-grey checked. The only touches of colour were the sashes round their gymslips – a different colour for each house – and the school badge, which was a black cat sitting on a yellow moon. For special occasions, such as prize-giving or Hallowe'en, there was another uniform consisting of a long robe worn with a tall, pointed hat, but as these were black too, it didn't really make much of a change.

There were so many rules that you couldn't do *any*thing without being told off, and there seemed to be tests and exams every week.

Mildred Hubble was in her first year at the school. She was one of those people who always seem to be in trouble. She didn't exactly mean to break rules and annoy the teachers, but things just seemed to *happen* whenever she was around. You could rely on Mildred to have her hat on back-to-front or her bootlaces trailing along the floor. She couldn't walk from one end of a corridor to the other without someone yelling at her, and nearly every night she was writing lines or being kept in (not that there was anywhere to go if you were allowed out). Anyway, she had lots of friends, even if they did keep their distance in the potion laboratory, and her best friend Maud stayed loyally by her through everything, however hair-raising. They made a funny pair, for Mildred was tall and thin with long plaits which she often chewed absent-mindedly (another thing she was told off about), while Maud was short and tubby, had round glasses and wore her hair in bunches.

On her first day at the academy each pupil was given a broomstick and taught to ride it, which takes quite a long time and isn't nearly as easy as it looks. Halfway through the first term they were each presented with a black kitten which they trained to ride the broomsticks. The cats weren't for any practical purpose except to keep tradition going; some schools present owls instead, but it's just a matter of taste. Miss Cackle was a very traditional headmistress who did not believe in any new-fangled nonsense and trained her young witches to keep up all the customs that had been taught in her young day. At the end of the first year, each pupil received a copy of *The Popular Book of Spells*, a three-inch thick volume bound in black leather. This was not really to be used as they already had paperback editions for the classroom, but like the cats it was another piece of tradition. Apart from yearly prize-giving, there were no more presentations until the fifth and final year when most pupils were awarded the Witches' Higher Certificate. It did not seem likely that Mildred would ever get that far. After only two days at the school she crashed her broomstick into the yard wall, breaking the broomstick in half and bending her hat. She mended the stick with glue and sticky-tape, and fortunately it still flew, though there was an ugly bundle where the ends joined and some-times it was rather difficult to control.

This story really begins halfway through Mildred's first term, on the night before the presentation of the kittens . . .

It was almost midnight and the school was in darkness except for one narrow window lit softly by the glow of a candle. This was Mildred's room where she was sitting in bed, wearing a pair of black-and-grey striped pyjamas and dropping off to sleep every few minutes. Maud was curled up on the end of the bed enveloped in a grey flannel nightdress and a black woollen shawl. Each pupil had the same type of room: very simple, with a wardrobe, iron bedstead, table and chair, and a slit window like the ones used by archers in castles of long ago. There was a picture rail along the bare walls from which hung a sampler embroidered with a quotation from *The Book of Spells* and also, during the day, several bats. Mildred had three bats in her room, little furry ones which were very friendly. She was fond of animals and was looking forward to the next day when she would have a kitten of her own. Everyone was very excited about the presentation, and they had all spent the evening ironing their best robes and pushing the dents out of their best hats. Maud was too excited to sleep, so had sneaked into Mildred's room to talk about it with her friend.

'What are you going to call yours, Maud?' asked Mildred, sleepily.

'Midnight,' said Maud. 'I think it sounds dramatic.'

'I'm worried about the whole thing,' Mildred confessed, chewing the end of her plait. 'I'm sure I'll do something dreadful like treading on its tail, or else it'll take one look at me and leap out of the window. *Some-thing's* bound to go wrong.'

'Don't be silly,' said Maud. 'You know you have a way with animals. And as for treading on its tail, it won't even be on the floor. Miss Cackle hands it to you, and that's all there is to it. So there's nothing to worry about, is there?'

Before Mildred had time to reply,

the door crashed open to reveal their form–mistress Miss Hardbroom standing in the doorway wrapped in a black dressing gown, with a lantern in her hand. She was a tall, terrifying lady with a sharp, bony face and black hair scragged back into such a tight knot that her forehead looked quite stretched.

'Rather late to be up, isn't it, girls?' she inquired nastily.

The girls, who had leapt into each other's arms when the door burst open, drew apart and fixed their eyes on the floor.

'Of course, if we don't want to be included in the presentation tomorrow we are certainly going about it the right way,' Miss Hardbroom continued icily.

'Yes, Miss Hardbroom,' chorused the girls miserably.

Miss Hardbroom glared meaningfully at Mildred's candle and swept out into the corridor with Maud in front of her.

Mildred hastily blew out the candle and dived under the bedclothes, but she could not get to sleep. Outside the window she could hear the owls hooting, and somewhere in the school a door had been left open and was creaking backwards and forwards in the wind. To tell you the truth, Mildred was afraid of the dark, but don't tell anyone. I mean, whoever heard of a *witch* who was scared of the dark?

CHAPTER 2

THE presentation took place in the Great Hall, a huge stone room with rows of wooden benches, a raised platform at one end and shields and portraits all round the walls. The whole school had assembled, and Miss Cackle, and Miss Hardbroom stood behind a table on the platform. On the table was a large wicker basket from which came mews and squeaks.

First of all everyone sang the school song, which went like this:

Onward, ever striving onward,
Proudly on our brooms we fly
Straight and true above the treetops,
Shadows on the moonlit sky.

Ne'er a day will pass before us
When we have not tried our best,
Kept our cauldrons bubbling nicely,
Cast our spells and charms with zest.

Full of joy we mix our potions,

Working by each other's side.
When our days at school are over
Let us think of them with pride.

It was the usual type of school song, full of pride, joy and striving. Mildred had never yet mixed a potion with joy, nor flown her broomstick with pride – she was usually too busy trying to keep upright!

Anyway, when they had finished droning the last verse, Miss Cackle rang the little silver bell on her table and the girls marched up in single file to receive their kittens. Mildred was the last of all, and when she reached the table Miss Cackle pulled out of the basket not a sleek black kitten like all the others but a little tabby with white paws and the sort of fur that looked as if it had been out all night in a gale.

'We ran out of black ones,' explained Miss Cackle with a pleasant grin.

Miss Hardbroom smiled too, but nastily.

After the ceremony everyone rushed to see Mildred's kitten.

'I think H.B. had a hand in this somewhere,' said Maud darkly. ('H.B.' was their nickname for Miss Hardbroom.)

'I must admit, it does look a bit dim, doesn't it?' said Mildred, scratching the tabby kitten's head. 'But I don't really mind. I'll just have to think of another name – I was going to call it Sooty. Let's take them down to the playground and see what they make of broomstick riding.'

Almost all the first-year witches were in the yard trying to persuade their puzzled kittens to sit on their broomsticks. Several were already clinging on by their claws, and one kitten, belonging to a rather smug young witch named Ethel, was sitting bolt upright cleaning its paws, as if it had been broomstick riding all its life!

Riding a broomstick was no easy matter, as I have mentioned before. First, you ordered the stick to hover, and it hovered lengthways above the ground. Then you sat on it, gave it a sharp tap, and away you flew. Once in the air you could make the stick do almost anything by saying, 'Right! Left! Stop! Down a bit!' and so on. The difficult part was balancing, for if you leaned a little too far to one side you could easily overbalance, in which case you would either fall off or find yourself hanging upside-down and then you would just have to hold on with your skirt over your head until a friend came to your rescue.

It had taken Mildred several weeks of falling off and crashing before she could ride the broomstick reasonably well, and it looked as though her kitten was going to have the same trouble. When she put it on the end of the stick, it just fell off without even trying to hold on. After many attempts, Mildred picked up her kitten and gave it a shake.

'Listen!' she said severely. 'I think I shall have to call you Stupid. You don't even *try* to hold on. Everyone else is all right – look at all your friends.'

The kitten gazed at her sadly and licked her nose with its rough tongue.

'Oh, come on,' said Mildred, softening her voice. 'I'm not really angry with you. Let's try again.'

And she put the kitten back on the broomstick, from which it fell with a thud.

Maud was having better luck. Her kitten was hanging on grimly upside down.

'Oh, well,' laughed Maud. 'It's a start.'

'Mine's useless,' said Mildred, sitting on the broomstick for a rest.

'Never mind,' Maud said. 'Think how hard it must be for them to hang on by their claws.'

An idea flashed into Mildred's head, and she dived into the school, leaving her kitten chasing a leaf along the ground and the broomstick still patiently hovering. She came out carrying her satchel which she hooked over the end of the broom and then bundled the kitten into it. The kitten's astounded face peeped out of the bag as Mildred flew delightedly round the yard.

'Look, Maud!' she called from ten feet up in the air.

'That's cheating!' said Maud, looking at the satchel.

Mildred flew back and landed on the ground laughing.

'I don't think H.B. will approve,' said Maud doubtfully.

'Quite right, Maud,' an icy voice behind them said. 'Mildred, my dear, possibly it would be even easier with handlebars and a saddle.'

Mildred blushed.

'I'm sorry, Miss Hardbroom,' she muttered. 'It doesn't balance very well – my kitten, so . . . I thought . . . perhaps . . .' Her voice trailed away under Miss Hardbroom's stony glare and Mildred unhooked her satchel and turned the bewildered kitten on to the ground.

'Girls!' Miss Hardbroom clapped her hands. 'I would remind you that there is a potion test tomorrow morning. That is all.'

So saying, she disappeared – literally.

'I wish she wouldn't do that,' whispered Maud, looking at the place where their form-mistress had been standing. 'You're never quite sure whether she's gone or not.'

'Right again, Maud,' came Miss Hardbroom's voice from nowhere.

Maud gulped and hurried back to her kitten.

CHAPTER 3

DO you remember I told you about a certain young witch named Ethel who had succeeded in teaching her kitten from the very first try? Ethel was one of those lucky people for whom everything goes right. She was always top of the class, her spells always worked, and Miss Hardbroom never made any icy remarks to her. Because of this, Ethel was often rather bossy with the other girls.

On this occasion she had overheard the whole of Mildred's encounter with Miss Hardbroom and couldn't resist being nasty about it.

'I think Miss Cackle gave you that cat on purpose,' Ethel sneered. 'You're both as bad as each other.'

'Oh, be quiet,' said Mildred, trying to keep her temper. 'Anyway, it's not a bad cat. It'll learn in time.'

'Like you did?' Ethel went on. 'Wasn't it last week that you crashed into the dustbins?'

'*Look*, Ethel,' Mildred said, 'you'd better be quiet, because if you don't I shall . . .'

'Well?'

'I shall have to turn you into a frog – and I don't want to do that.'

Ethel gave a shriek of laughter.

'That's really funny!' she crowed. 'You don't even know the beginners' spells, let alone ones like that.'

Mildred blushed and looked very miserable.

'Go on, then!' cried Ethel. 'Go *on*, then, if you're so clever. *Turn* me into a frog! I'm waiting.'

It just so happened that Mildred did have an idea of that spell (she had been reading about it in the library). By now, everyone had crowded round, waiting to see what would happen, and Ethel was still jeering. It was unbearable.

Mildred muttered the spell under her breath – and Ethel vanished. In her place stood a small pink and grey pig.

Cries and shouts rent the air:

'Oh, no!'

'That's torn it!'

'You've done it now, Mildred!'

Mildred was horrified. 'Oh, Ethel,' she said. 'I'm sorry, but you did ask for it.'

The pig looked furious.

'You *beast*, Mildred Hubble!' it grunted. 'Change me back!'

At that moment Miss Hardbroom suddenly appeared in the middle of the yard.

'Where is Ethel Hallow?' she asked. 'Miss Bat would like to see her about extra chanting lessons.'

Her sharp gaze fell on the small pig which was grunting softly at her feet.

'What is this animal doing in the yard?' she asked, coldly.

Everyone looked at Mildred.

'I . . . let it in, Miss Hardbroom,' Mildred said hesitantly.

'Well, you can just let it out again, please,' said Miss Hardbroom.

'Oh, I can't do that!' gasped the unhappy Mildred. 'I mean, well . . . er . . . Couldn't I keep it as a pet?'

'I think you have quite enough trouble coping with yourself and that kitten without adding a pig to your worries,' replied Miss Hardbroom, staring at the tabby kitten which was peering round Mildred's ankles. 'Let it out at once! Now, where is Ethel?'

Mildred bent down.

'Ethel, dear,' she whispered coaxingly in the pig's ear. 'Will you go out when I tell you to? Please, Ethel, I'll let you in again straight away afterwards.'

Pleading with people like Ethel never works. It only makes them feel their power.

'I *won't* go !' bellowed the pig. 'Miss Hardbroom, I *am* Ethel! Mildred Hubble turned me into a pig.'

Nothing ever surprised Miss Hardbroom. Even this startling piece of news only caused her to raise one slanting eyebrow.

'Well, Mildred,' she said, 'I am glad to know that you have at least learned *one* thing since you came here. However, as you will have noticed in the Witches' Code, rule number seven, paragraph two, it is not customary to practise such tricks on your fellows. Please remove the spell at once.'

'I'm afraid I don't know how to,' Mildred confessed, in a very small voice.

Miss Hardbroom stared at her for a few moments.

'Then you had better go and look it up in the library,' she said, wearily. 'Take Ethel with you, and on your way drop in and tell Miss Bat why Ethel will be late.'

Mildred picked up her kitten and

hurried inside, followed by the pig. Fortunately, Miss Bat was not in her room, but it was most embarrassing going into the library. Ethel was grunting loudly on purpose and everyone stared so much that Mildred could have crawled under the table.

'Hurry up,' moaned the pig.

'Oh, stop going on!' said Mildred, as she flicked hastily through the huge spell book. 'It's all your fault, anyway. You actually *asked* me to do it. I don't see why you're complaining.'

'I said a frog, not a pig,' said Ethel, pettily. 'You couldn't even do *that* right.'

Mildred ignored the grunting Ethel and kept looking in the book. It took her half an hour to find the right spell, and soon after that Ethel was her horrible self again. The people in the library were most surprised to see the pig suddenly change into a furious-looking Ethel.

'Now, don't be angry, Ethel,' Mildred said softly. 'Remember: "Silence in the library at all times".'

And she rushed into the corridor.

'Wasn't that awful, Cat?' she said to the kitten, which was curled up inside her cardigan. 'I think I'd better put you in my room and then go and revise for the potion test. Don't tease the bats, will you?'

CHAPTER 4

IT was the morning of the potion test and the girls were filing into the potion lab, each hoping she had learned the right spell, except for Ethel who knew everything and never worried about such matters.

'Come along, girls! Two to a cauldron!' barked Miss Hardbroom. 'Today we shall make a laughter potion. No textbooks to be used – put that book away this *instant*, Mildred! Work quietly, and when you have finished you may take a small sip of the mixture to make sure it is correctly made. You may begin.'

Maud and Mildred were sharing a cauldron, of course, but unfortunately neither of them had learned that particular spell.

'I think I can remember it vaguely,' whispered Maud. 'Bits of it, anyway.' She began to sort through the ingredients which had been laid out on each workbench.

When everything was stirred together in the cauldron, the bubbling liquid was bright pink. Mildred stared at it doubtfully.

'I'm sure it should be green,' she said. 'In fact I'm sure we should have put in a handful of pondweed-gathered-at-midnight.'

'Are you *sure*?' asked Maud.

'Yes . . .' replied Mildred, not very definitely.

'*Absolutely* sure?' Maud asked again. 'You know what happened last time.'

'I'm *quite* sure,' insisted Mildred. 'Anyway, there's a handful of pondweed laid out on each bench. I'm positive we're supposed to put it in.'

'Oh, all right,' said Maud. 'Go on, then. It can't do any harm.'

Mildred grabbed the pondweed and dropped it into the mixture. They took turns at stirring it for a few minutes until it began to turn dark green.

'What a horrid colour,' said Maud.

'Are you ready, girls?' asked Miss Hardbroom, rapping on her desk. 'You should have been ready minutes ago. A laughter potion should be made quickly for use in an emergency.'

Ethel was still working on the bench in front of Mildred, who stood on tiptoe to sneak a look at the colour of Ethel's potion. To her horror, it was bright pink.

'Oh, no,' Mildred thought, with a sinking feeling. 'I wonder what potion we've made?'

Miss Hardbroom banged on the desk again.

'We shall now test the potion,' she commanded. 'Not too much, please. We don't want anyone hysterical.'

Each pupil took a test-tubeful of liquid and drank a little. At once shrieks of laughter rang through the room, especially from Ethel's bench where they had made the best potion of all and were laughing so much that tears rolled down their cheeks. The only two girls who weren't laughing were Mildred and Maud.

'Oh, dear,' said Maud. 'I feel most peculiar. Why aren't we laughing, Mil?'

'I hate to tell you,' confessed Mildred, 'I think —' But before she had time to say any more, the two girls had disappeared!

'Cauldron number two!' snapped Miss Hardbroom. 'You seem to have made the wrong spell.'

'It was my fault,' said Mildred's voice from behind the cauldron.

'That I do not doubt,' Miss Hardbroom said sourly. 'You had both better sit down until you reappear, and then, Mildred, perhaps a trip to Miss Cackle's office would do you some good. You can explain why I sent you.'

Everyone had left the room by the time the two young witches finally began to reappear. This was a very slow process, with first the head and then the rest of the body becoming gradually visible.

'I'm sorry,' said Mildred's head and shoulders.

'That's all right,' said Maud's head. 'I just wish you'd *think* a bit more. We had the right potion to start with.'

'Sorry,' mumbled Mildred again, then she began to laugh. 'Hey, Maud, you do look funny with just your head showing!'

At once they both began to laugh, and soon they were best friends again.

'I suppose I'd better go and see Old Cackle now,' said Mildred, when she had completely reappeared.

'I'll come with you to the door,' offered Maud.

Miss Cackle was small and very fat, with short grey hair and green horn-rimmed glasses which she usually wore pushed up on top of her head. She was the exact opposite of Miss Hardbroom, being absent-minded in appearance and rather gentle by nature. The girls were not in the least bit afraid of her, whereas Miss Hardbroom could reduce any of them to a miserable heap with just one word. Miss Cackle used a different technique. By always being friendly and pleased to see a pupil in her office, she made them feel embarrassed if they had something unpleasant to tell her, as Mildred nearly always had.

Mildred knocked at Miss Cackle's door hoping she would be out. She wasn't.

'Come in!' called the familiar voice from inside.

Mildred opened the door and went in. Miss Cackle, glasses on her nose for once was busily writing in a huge register. She looked up and peered over her spectacles.

'Ah, Mildred,' she said pleasantly. 'Come and sit down while I finish filling in this register.'

Mildred closed the door and sat by Miss Cackle's desk.

'I wish she wasn't so pleased to see me,' she thought.

Miss Cackle slammed the register shut and pushed her glasses on to the top of her head.

'Now, Mildred, what can I do for you?'

Mildred twisted her fingers together.

'Well, actually, Miss Cackle,' she began slowly, 'Miss Hardbroom sent me to see you because I made the wrong potion again.'

The smile faded from the headmistress's face and she sighed, as if with deep disappointment. Mildred felt about an inch high.

'*Really*, Mildred,' Miss Cackle said in a tired voice, 'I have run out of things to say to you. Week after week you come here, sent by every member of staff in the school, and my words just seem to go straight in one ear and out of the other. You will never get the Witches' Higher Certificate if this appalling conduct continues. You must be the worst witch in the entire school. Whenever there's any trouble you are nearly always to be found at the bottom of it, and it's just not good enough, my dear. Now, what have you to say for yourself *this* time?'

'I don't really know, Miss Cackle,' Mildred said humbly. 'Everything I do just seems to go wrong, that's all. I don't *mean* to do it.'

'Well, that's no excuse, is it?' said Miss Cackle. 'Everyone else manages to live without causing an uproar wherever they go. You must pull yourself together Mildred. I don't want to hear anymore bad reports about you, do you understand?'

'Yes, Miss Cackle,' said Mildred, in as sorry a voice as she could manage.

'Run along, then,' said the head-mistress, 'and remember what I have said to you.'

Maud was waiting in the corridor, eager to know what had been said, when her friend came out of the office.

'She's nice really,' Mildred said. 'Just told me all the usual things. She hates telling people off. I'll have to try to be better from now on. Come on, let's go and give the kittens another broomstick lesson.'

CHAPTER 5

THE following morning, Miss Hardbroom strode into the classroom looking thoughtful. She was wearing a new grey-and-black striped dress, with a brooch at the shoulder.

'Good morning, girls,' she greeted them, not as sharply as usual.

'Good morning, Miss Hardbroom,' chorused the girls.

Their form-mistress arranged the books on her desk and surveyed the class.

'I have something to tell you, girls,' she began, 'that gives me great pleasure on one hand, yet causes me some worry on the other.' Here she shot a glance at Mildred. 'As you know, the Hallowe'en celebrations take place in two weeks' time and it is customary for a display to be presented by this school. This year, our class has been chosen to present the display.'

There were gasps of delight from the girls.

'Of course,' Miss Hardbroom went on, 'it is a great honour, but also a responsibility, as Miss Cackle's Academy has a very high reputation which we don't want to spoil, *do we*? Last year, Form Three produced a play which was highly praised, and I thought that this year we might present a broomstick formation team. You will need a lot of practice, as some of you are not too steady on your broomsticks yet, but I am quite certain that we could give an interesting and successful performance. Is there anyone who would prefer something different?'

She looked round piercingly at the girls, who all shrank into their seats and would not have dared to disagree, even if they had wanted to.

'Good,' said Miss Hardbroom. 'Then it is settled. We shall present a broomstick formation team. Let us go down to the yard and begin to practise at once. Fetch your broomsticks and be outside in two minutes.' With which words she vanished.

The girls excitedly clattered from the room and rushed along the corridors to fetch their broomsticks, which were kept in their own rooms. The spiral staircase rang with the sound of hob-nailed boots as the girls rushed down to the yard, where they found Miss Hardbroom waiting for them.

'First of all, you'd better take a practice flight,' she said. 'Form an orderly crocodile and go round the school and back.'

Off they all flew in an orderly, but rather wobbly, procession round the school.

'Quite good, girls,' said Miss Hardbroom, as they lined up in front of her. 'You were swaying about rather badly, Mildred, but apart from that, you all did quite well. Now, I have made out a list of the things you will be doing. First, a single line, with each pupil sinking and rising alternately. This should be comparatively easy. Secondly, a flying "V" similar to wild geese in flight. Then, nose-diving the yard, and swooping up just before you reach the ground. That will be the most difficult part of all.' Mildred and Maud exchanged horrified glances. 'And finally you will form a circle in the air, each broomstick touching the next. Any questions? No? Very well, then, we shall begin the first item immediately. What *was* the first item, Mildred?'

'. . . er, nose-diving the yard, Miss Hardbroom.'

'Wrong. Ethel, do you remember?'

'We are to form a line, each pupil sinking and rising alternately,' replied Ethel, word-perfect as always.

'Correct,' said Miss Hardbroom, with a frosty glare at Mildred. 'We shall practise all this morning and every morning until the celebrations, and perhaps this afternoon, if I can persuade Miss Bat to allow you to miss your chanting lesson.'

They worked very hard for the next two weeks. Every spare minute was spent practising and, by the time Hallowe'en arrived, the display was quite a joy to watch. Maud's hat was squashed like a concertina from the time when she had not pulled up from a nose-dive during practice, but apart from that there had been hardly any trouble at all, even from Mildred, who was making a special effort to be good and thoughtful.

The day before Hallowe'en, Miss Hardbroom lined up her class in the yard to give them a few final words of advice.

'I am very pleased with you, girls,' she said, almost pleasantly. 'Now, you will be wearing your best robes tomorrow, so I hope they will be clean and pressed.'

As she said this she caught sight of Mildred's broomstick.

'Mildred, why is there a bundle of sticky-tape in the middle of your broomstick?'

'I'm afraid I broke it in half during the first week of term,' admitted Mildred.

Ethel giggled.

'I see,' said Miss Hardbroom. 'Well, you certainly can't use that one in the display. Ethel, I seem to remember you have a spare one. Perhaps you could lend it to Mildred?'

'Oh, Miss Hardbroom!' cried Ethel. 'It was given to me as a birthday present. I shouldn't want anything to happen to it.'

Miss Hardbroom fixed Ethel with one of her nastiest looks.

'If that is how you feel, Ethel,' she said in icy tones, 'then –'

'Oh, I didn't mean I *won't* lend it, Miss Hardbroom,' Ethel said, meekly. 'I'll go and fetch it now.' And she ran into the school.

Ethel had never forgotten the time Mildred had turned her into a pig, and as she made her way up the spiral staircase she suddenly thought of a marvellous way of taking her revenge. (Ethel really wasn't a nice person at all.)

'I'll fix you, Mildred Hubble,' she cackled to herself, as she took the broomstick out of her cupboard. 'Now, listen to me, Broom, this is very important . . .'

The class had dismissed when Ethel returned carrying the broomstick. Mildred was practising nose-diving the yard.

'Here's the broom, Mildred,' called Ethel. 'I'll leave it propped against the wall.'

'Thanks very much,' replied Mildred, delighted that Ethel was being so nice, for the two hadn't spoken since the pig episode. 'It's very kind of you.'

'Not at all,' said Ethel, smiling wickedly to herself as she went back into the school.

CHAPTER 6

HALLOWE'EN was celebrated each year in the ruins of an old castle quite near the school. The special fires were lit at sunset, and by dark all the witches and wizards had assembled.

As the sun set, the members of Miss Cackle's Academy were preparing to leave the school. Mildred smoothed her robes, said good-bye to her kitten, put on her hat, grabbed Ethel's broomstick and ran down to the yard. She took a quick look out of her window before leaving the room and saw the fires being lit in the distance. It was very exciting.

The rest of the school had already assembled as Mildred rushed out of the door and took her place. Miss Hardbroom looked splendid in her full witch's robes and hat.

'Everyone is present now,' Miss

Hardbroom announced to Miss Cackle.

'Then we shall set off,' said the headmistress. 'To the celebrations! Class Five first, Class Four second, and so on until Class One!'

They made a wonderful sight flying over the trees towards the castle, cloaks soaring in the wind, and the older girls with their cats perched on the ends of their broomsticks. Miss Hardbroom looked particularly impressive, sitting bolt-upright with her long black hair streaming behind her. The girls had never seen her hair loose before and were amazed how much of it she could possibly scrag into that tight knot every day. It came down to her waist.

'H.B. looks quite nice with her hair like that,' whispered Maud to Mildred, who was riding next to her.

'Yes,' agreed Mildred, 'she doesn't seem half as frightening.'

Miss Hardbroom turned round and shot a piercing look at the two girls.

'No talking!' she snapped.

A huge crowd was already there at the castle when they arrived. The pupils of the Academy lined up in neat rows while Miss Cackle and all the other teachers shook hands with the chief wizard. He was very old, with a long white beard and a purple gown embroidered with moons and stars.

'And what have you prepared for us this year?' he asked.

'We have prepared a broomstick formation team, Your Honour,' Miss Cackle replied. 'Shall we begin, Miss Hardbroom?'

Miss Hardbroom clapped her hands and the girls lined up, with Ethel at the front.

'You may begin,' said Miss Hardbroom.

Ethel rose perfectly into the air, followed by the rest of the class. First, they made a line, sinking and rising, which received great applause. Then they nose-dived the yard. Miss Cackle closed her eyes during this part, but nothing went wrong. Then the girls made a V in the air, which looked quite beautiful.

'Your girls get better every year,'

remarked a young witch to Miss Hardbroom, who smiled.

Last of all came the circle, which
was quite the easiest part.

'All over soon,' whispered Maud,
arranging her broomstick in front of
Mildred.

As soon as they had formed the
circle, Mildred knew that something
was the matter with her broomstick.
It started to rock about, and seemed
to be trying to throw her off balance.

'Maud!' she cried to her friend.
'There's something —' but before
Mildred could say any more, the
broomstick gave a violent kick like
a bucking bronco and she fell off,
grabbing at Maud as she fell.

There was chaos in the air. All the

girls were screaming and clutching at each other, and soon there was a tangled mass of broomsticks and witches on the ground. The only girl who flew serenely back to earth was Ethel. A few of the younger witches laughed, but most of them looked grim.

'We are so sorry, Your Honour,' apologized Miss Cackle, as Miss Hardbroom untangled the heap of girls and jerked them to their feet. 'I'm sure there must be some simple explanation.'

'Miss Cackle,' said the chief magician sternly, 'your pupils are the witches of the future. I shudder to think what that future will be like.'

He paused, and there was complete

silence. Miss Hardbroom glared at Mildred.

'However,' continued the chief magician, 'we shall forget this incident for the rest of the evening. Let us now begin the chanting.'

CHAPTER 7

AT dawn the celebrations ended, and the pupils flew wearily back to school, some riding double as their own broomsticks were broken. No one was speaking to Mildred (even Maud was being very cool towards her friend), and Form One was in disgrace. When they arrived at the Academy, everyone was sent straight to bed. It was the custom, after the all-night Hallowe'en celebrations, to sleep until noon the next day.

'Mildred!' said Miss Cackle, in a sharp voice, as Form One made their way miserably up the stairs. 'Miss Hardbroom and I will see you in my office first thing tomorrow afternoon.'

'Yes, Miss Cackle,' replied Mildred, almost in tears, and she ran up the steps.

As Mildred opened her bedroom door, Ethel, who was behind her, leaned across and whispered, '*That*'ll teach you to go around changing people into pigs!' and she pulled a face and ran away down the corridor.

Mildred closed the door and fell on to her bed, almost flattening the kitten which leapt out of the way just in time.

'Oh, Tabby,' she said, burying her face in the kitten's warm fur, 'I've had such a dreadful time, and it wasn't even my fault! I might have known Ethel wouldn't lend me her broomstick out of kindness. Nobody will ever believe that it wasn't me just being clumsy as usual.'

The kitten licked her ear sympathetically, and the bats returned through the narrow window and settled upside down on the picture-rail.

Two hours later, Mildred was lying in bed, still wide awake. She was imagining what the interview with Miss Cackle and her terrible form-mistress would be like. The kitten was curled up peacefully on her chest.

'It'll be awful,' she thought, sadly looking towards the grey sky outside the window. 'I wonder if they'll expel me? Or perhaps I could tell them that it was Ethel – no, I would never do that. Suppose they decided to turn me into a frog? No, I'm sure they wouldn't do anything like that; Miss Hardbroom said that was against the Witches' Code. Oh, what *will* they do to me? Even Maud thinks it's my fault, and I've never seen H.B. look more furious.'

She lay thinking about it until she was really frightened, and suddenly she leapt out of bed.

'Come on, Tabby!' she said, pulling a bag out of the wardrobe. 'We're running away.'

She stuffed a few clothes and books into the bag and put on her best robe so that no one would recognize the usual school uniform. Then she picked up her broomstick, put the kitten into the bag, and crept out along the silent corridor to the spiral staircase.

'I shall miss the bats,' she thought.

It was a cold, dull morning, and Mildred pulled her cape about her shoulders as she crossed the yard, glancing round in case anyone was watching. The school seemed very strange with no one about. Mildred had to fly over the gates, which were locked as usual, but it was difficult to balance with the bag slung on the back of her broomstick, so she got off on the other side of the gates and started through the pine trees on foot.

'I don't know where we're going, Tabby,' she said, as they picked their way down the mountainside.

CHAPTER 8

IT was very gloomy in the forest, and Mildred felt slightly uneasy, surrounded by dark trees which grew so thickly together that no light fell between them. When she was almost at the bottom of the mountain, she sat down to rest, leaning her back against a tree, and the kitten climbed out of the bag to stretch itself on the grass.

It was very quiet except for a few birds singing, and a rather strange noise, a sort of low humming, almost like a lot of people talking at once. In fact, the more Mildred listened, the more it did sound like voices. She looked in the direction of the noise and thought she saw something moving along the trees.

'Let's go and have a look, Tabby,' she whispered.

They left the bag and broomstick leaning against the tree, and crept through the tangled undergrowth. The noise grew louder.

'Why, it *is* people talking,' said Mildred. 'Look, Tabby, over there, through the branches.'

Sitting in a clearing in the gloom were about twenty witches, all crowded together, muttering and talking in low voices. Mildred crept nearer and listened. She didn't recognize any of them. A tall, grey-haired witch got to her feet.

'Listen, everyone,' said the grey-haired witch. 'Will you all be quiet for a few moments? Thank you. Now what I should like to know is, are we quite sure that they will all be sleeping, or at least in their rooms?'

She sat down, and another witch got up to reply. She was a small, plump witch with green horn-rimmed glasses. For a horrible moment Mildred thought it was Miss Cackle, but her voice was different when she spoke.

'Of course we are sure,' this witch replied. 'The morning after Hallowe'en celebrations the entire school sleeps until midday. It is a rule, and the school is very strict about rules, so no one will be up until five minutes to twelve at the very earliest. If we fly over the wall into the back part of the yard, we will be as far away from the bedrooms as we can be, and no one will possibly hear us. Added to this, we shall all be invisible, so we shall be extremely well protected. Then all that remains to be done is to split up, sneak into each room and turn them all into frogs. They won't be able to see us even if they *are* awake. Remember to take one of these boxes with you for the frogs.' She pointed to a neat pile of small cardboard boxes. 'We can't have even one of them escaping. Once this is done, the entire school and everyone in it will be under our control.

'Is the invisibility potion ready yet?' she continued, turning to a young witch who was stirring a cauldron over a fire. It was the same potion that the two Ms had made during the laughter potion test.

'Another few minutes,' replied the young witch, dropping a handful of bats' whiskers into the mixture. 'It needs to simmer for a bit.'

Mildred was horrified. She sneaked back to where she had left her bag, and then into the shadows so that she couldn't be seen.

'What on earth can we do, Tab?' she whispered to the kitten, imagining Maud hopping about turned into a frog. 'We can't let them take over the school.'

She rummaged through the bag and took out the two books she had brought with her. One was the Witches' Code and the other was her spell book. Mildred flicked through the spell book and stopped at the page about turning people into animals. There was only one example given, and that was snails.

'Dare I?' thought Mildred. 'Dare

I turn the whole lot of them into snails? The kitten looked at her, encouragingly.

'I know it's against the Witches' Code, Tabby,' she said, 'but *they* don't seem to follow any rules. They were planning to change us into frogs while we were *asleep* so I don't see why we shouldn't do the same to them in self-defence.'

She sneaked back to the clearing clutching her spell book.

'Here goes!' she thought desperately.

The invisibility potion was being poured out into cups, so Mildred had to work quickly. She waved her arms in a circle towards the crowd of witches (this part of spell-making can be very awkward when you don't want to draw attention to yourself) and muttered the spell under her breath. For a second, nothing happened, and the witches milling round the cauldron continued to chatter and bustle about. Mildred closed her eyes in despair, but when she opened them again everyone had vanished and on the ground was a group of snails of all different shapes and sizes.

'Tabby!' shrieked Mildred. 'I've done it! Look!'

Tabby came bounding out of the undergrowth and stared at the snails, who were all moving away as fast as they could, which wasn't very fast. Mildred took one of the cardboard boxes and put the snails into it, gently picking them up one by one.

'I suppose we'll have to take them back to school and tell Miss Cackle, Tab,' she said, suddenly remembering her interview to come at noon. 'Still, we'll have to go back. We can't just leave this lot here, can we?'

So they set off up the mountainside, Mildred carrying the box in her arms while the broomstick flew alongside with the bag hanging from it and Tabby riding inside the bag.

CHAPTER 9

THE school was still completely
deserted when Mildred ar-
rived once more at the heavy
iron gates. She hurried up the
spiral staircase to her room and un-
packed her bag so that no one would

know she had tried to run away. Just as she was making her way to the door with the box in her arms, the door opened and Miss Hardbroom appeared.

'Would you kindly tell me what you are doing, Mildred?' she asked frostily. 'I have just watched you creeping up the corridor, complete with broomstick, cat, a bag and this cardboard box. Is it too much to ask for an explanation?'

'Oh, no, Miss Hardbroom,' replied Mildred, holding up the box for her form mistress to see the contents. 'You see, I found a crowd of witches on the mountainside, and they were planning to take over the school and change you all into frogs, and they were making an invisibility potion so you wouldn't be able to see them, so I turned them all into snails and brought . . .'

Her words trailed into silence as she saw the expression on Miss Hardbroom's face. Obviously, her form-mistress didn't believe a word.

'I suppose these are the witches?' she asked bitterly, pointing to the snails which were all huddled up in one corner of the box.

'Yes, they are!' Mildred insisted desperately. 'I know it sounds a peculiar story, Miss Hardbroom, but you must believe me. Their broomsticks and cauldrons and things are still in the clearing where I found them, really.'

'Well, you had better show the creatures to Miss Cackle,' said Miss Hard-broom, nastily. 'Go and wait in Miss Cackle's Office while I fetch her — and I hope this isn't any sort of joke, Mildred. I seem to remember that you are already in a considerable amount of trouble.'

Mildred was perched nervously on the edge off a chair in the head-mistress's office when Miss Hard-broom returned with Miss Cackle, who was wearing a grey dressing-gown, and looked half asleep.

'*These* are they,' stated Miss Hard-broom, pointing to the box on the desk.

Miss Cackle sat down heavily in her chair and looked first into the box and then at Mildred.

'Mildred,' she said in dramatic tones, 'I am still suffering from my public humiliation last night. Because of you the reputation of this school now lies in the mud, and yet you expect me to believe an incredible story like this?'

'But it's *true*!' cried Mildred. 'I can even describe some of them. One was tall and thin with thick grey hair, and there was another who looked just like you, Miss Cackle, if you'll excuse me being personal. She had green horn-rimmed glasses –'

'Wait a moment!' said Miss Cackle, pushing her own glasses on to her nose. 'Did you say she had horn-rimmed glasses and looked like me?'

'Yes, Miss Cackle,' replied Mildred,

blushing. 'Green ones. I'm sorry if you thought I was being rude.'

'No, no, child, it isn't that,' said Miss Cackle, peering into the box again. Then she turned to Miss Hardbroom. 'Do you know, I think the girl may be right after all. The person whom she described sounds exactly like my wicked sister Agatha who has always been extremely jealous of my position at this Academy!'

Miss Cackle stared over her glasses at the snails.

'Well, well, Agatha,' she chuckled. 'So we meet again. I wonder which of these beauties you are? What shall we do with them, Miss Hardbroom?'

'I suggest we change them back to their natural form again.'

'But we can't!' cried Miss Cackle in dismay. 'There are *twenty* of them.'

Miss Hardbroom looked faintly amused.

'May I point out,' she said, 'paragraph five of rule number seven in the Witches' Code, which states that anyone having been changed into any type of animal by another witch, for purposes of self-defence, cannot, on being changed back again, practise any form of magic against their captor. In other words, they must admit defeat.'

Miss Cackle looked embarrassed.

'Oh, yes!' she said brightly. 'I remember now. It slipped my mind for the moment. Did you hear that, Agatha? Do you think they can hear us, Miss Hardbroom?'

'Most certainly,' replied Miss Hard-broom. 'Perhaps you could line them up on your desk, and ask your sister to step forward?'

'What a splendid idea,' said Miss Cackle, who was beginning to enjoy herself. 'Help me, Mildred, my dear.'

They lined the snails up on the desk and Miss Cackle asked Agatha to step forward. One snail shuffled rather reluctantly out of line.

'Listen, Agatha,' said Miss Cackle. 'You must admit that you don't really have much choice. If you will agree to abide by the Witches' Code, then we can change you back, but not otherwise. If you agree, go back into line so that we know what you want us to do.'

The snail shuffled back into line again.

Miss Hardbroom spoke the words of the spell which released them, and suddenly the room was full of witches, all looking furious and talking angrily at the same time. The noise was terrible.

'Will you be quiet at once!' commanded Miss Cackle.

She turned to Mildred who was still perched on her chair. 'You may go back to bed, Mildred, and in view of what you have done for the school this morning, I think we will have to forget about the interview you were to have had with Miss Hardbroom and myself this afternoon. Don't you agree, Miss Hardbroom?'

Miss Hardbroom raised one eye-brow and Mildred's heart sank.

'Before I agree, Miss Cackle, if you'll forgive me,' she said, 'I would just like to ask Mildred what she was doing wandering about on the mountain when she should have been in bed?'

'I – I was out for a walk, Miss Hardbroom,' replied Mildred.

'And you just happened to have your spell book with you.'

'Yes,' agreed Mildred, unhappily.

'Such devotion to the school!' said Miss Hardbroom, smiling in a most unpleasant way. 'Taking your spell book with you wherever you go. I expect you were also singing the school song as you rambled along, weren't you, my dear?'

Mildred looked at the floor. She could feel all the other witches staring at her.

'I think we must let the child go to bed,' said Miss Cackle. 'Run along now, Mildred.'

Mildred shot out of the room before her form-mistress could say anything else, and was in bed in five seconds!

CHAPTER 10

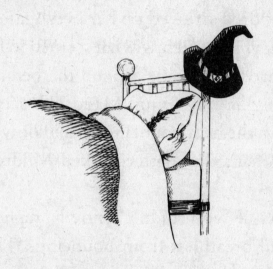

AT noon the rising bell clanged through the corridors but Mildred pulled the pillow over her head and went back to sleep. It wasn't long before the door of her room burst open.

'Wake up, Mildred!' shrieked Maud, seizing the pillow and hitting her friend over the head with it.

Mildred screwed up her eyes against the daylight and saw what seemed to be hundreds of people around the bed all talking and shouting. Maud was actually *on* the bed, bouncing up and down.

'What's the matter?' asked Mildred sleepily.

'As if you didn't know!' replied Maud breathless from bouncing. 'The whole school's talking about it.'

'About what?' said Mildred, who was still half-asleep.

'*Will* you wake up?' shrieked Maud pulling the bedclothes back. 'You saved the whole school from Miss Cackle's wicked sister, that's all!'

Mildred sat bolt upright.

'So I did!' she exclaimed, and everyone laughed.

'Miss Cackle's called a meeting in the Great Hall,' said Dawn and Gloria, two other members of Form One. 'You'd better hurry and dress, she'll expect you to be there.'

Mildred jumped out of bed and her friends went off to the hall. She was soon ready and ran to join them, shoelaces trailing along the floor as usual.

Maud had saved a place for her, and Mildred was embarrassed to notice that everyone stared as she came into the hall. While they waited for the teachers to arrive, Mildred decided to tell her friend about Ethel.

'Listen,' she whispered, leaning towards Maud so that no one could hear. 'It wasn't my fault about the display. Ethel cast a spell on the broomstick that she lent me, and I know because she told me. Don't tell anyone else, will you? But I wanted you to know because I don't want you thinking that I was just being clumsy.'

'But everyone already knows,' said Maud.

'Do they?' exclaimed Mildred. 'Who told them?'

'Well, you know what Ethel's like,' replied Maud. 'She just had to tell someone how clever she'd been so she told Harriet, and Harriet thought it was a dreadful thing to do so *she* told everyone else. No one's talking to Ethel now and Miss Hardbroom found out too and was furious with her.'

'Shhhhh!' said someone. 'They're coming.'

Everyone stood up as Miss Cackle came in, followed by Miss Hardbroom and all the other teachers.

'You may sit down, girls,' said the headmistress. 'As you all know, the school narrowly escaped invasion this morning. Had it not been for a certain young member of the school we should not be here but would be hopping about turned into frogs.'

The girls laughed.

'No, no, girls! Do not laugh! It would not be at all funny had it happened. However, as it did *not* happen,

I proclaim the rest of today a half holiday in honour of Mildred Hubble. Mildred, would you come up here for a moment?'

Mildred went bright red and was pushed to her feet. She stumbled through the rows of chairs, tripping over feet as she went, and clumped across the platform to Miss Cackle's table.

'Now don't be shy, my dear,' said Miss Cackle beaming. She turned to the school. 'Come along, school! Three cheers for our heroine Mildred.'

Mildred blushed and twisted her fingers behind her back as the cheers rang out.

It was a relief to the 'heroine' when it was all over. As they filed out of

the hall she was thumped on the back
and congratulated by everyone –
except for Ethel who gave Mildred
the nastiest look you've ever seen.

'Good old Mil!' yelled someone.

'We'll get out of our chanting test,
thanks to you,' said someone else.

'Thanks for the holiday!'

'Thanks, Mil!' And so on.

Maud flung an arm around her
friend.

'You did look embarrassed,' she
said. 'You went ever so red, I could
see you from the back of the hall!'

'Oh, *don't*,' said Mildred. 'Let's go
and fetch the kittens and make the
most of our holiday.'

'One moment,' said a chilling voice
that they knew so well. The two girls

turned to find their form-mistress standing behind them. They jumped to attention at once, wondering what they had done which was a natural reaction whenever Miss Hardbroom spoke.

This time, however, to their amazement, she smiled, a friendly smile not like the usual curl at the corner of the lips.

'I just wanted to say thank you Mildred,' she said. 'Run along now, girls and enjoy your holiday before it's over.'

She smiled again and vanished.

The girls just stared at each other.

'Sometimes,' said Mildred, 'I think she probably isn't as mean as we think she is.

'Perhaps you are right, Mildred,' said Miss Hardbroom's voice from behind Mildred's ear, and the two girls jumped in horror!

Mildred grabbed her friend's hand and they hurried away down the corridor out into the misty playground leaving Miss Hardbroom's laughter echoing from nowhere along the empty passage.

AFTERWORD

It is not surprising that Jill Murphy knew what little girls would enjoy reading – she was eighteen when she wrote *The Worst Witch*, and had only recently been a little girl herself. But after three publishers (adults, of course) had told her it was boring, she put it away for six years. Now the enormous success of the book has proved that she was right and they were wrong.

What is surprising, however, and what continues to puzzle adults, is *why* young readers love it so much. The answer at first looks easy. It's a deliciously comic version of the classic school story, but one where wildly fantastic events are carried out by very human characters treating their magical powers in an offhand, down-to-earth sort of way. School, magic and humour: the combination is irresistible.

Who wouldn't long to turn their worst enemy into a pig? Who has never felt that everything they do turns out wrong, that teachers always seem to appear at the wrong moment, and always misunderstand? So how comforting to picture young witches feeling the same way – but with the power to do something about it!

As many other witch stories have shown, it is more fun, and even more comforting, to watch witches make mistakes before they quite manage to get it right. But in those stories the witches are usually horrid cackling old women, so it's surprising, funny and rather nice to think of them as little schoolgirls who are still learning, taking tests, being ticked off and having to listen to the same old phrases like anyone else: 'Two to a cauldron!' barked Miss Hardbroom . . . 'Work quietly . . . Are you ready, girls? You should have been ready minutes ago . . .'

Jill Murphy sets all this magic into a story of the immortal Chalet School type. Miss Cackle's Academy is a girls' boarding-school built at the top, in-stead of the bottom, of a pine-forested mountain. It is strict and traditional (based on Jill Murphy's memories of her own convent school), and its school song is a perfect parody, a funny imitation, of all the stirring old-fashioned kinds. Our heroine Mildred, tall and gangling with long plaits, is the complete opposite of Maud, bespectacled, short and tubby – as the best friends of such stories always are. Even the names, Mildred, Maud, Ethel, which are quaint today, are the perfectly normal ones of old books.

All the familiar ingredients of the boarding-school adventure are here: the horrid, smug swot who gets her come-uppance; a code of honour, because even when Mildred realizes

Ethel is the guilty one, she accepts her punishment rather than tell tales; the ferocious teacher who might be quite decent underneath; being sent to the Head; the unfair accusation, and running away. When Mildred uncovers an evil plot, and warns the school instead of escaping, just listen to the echoes of all those classic stories! 'I proclaim the rest of today a holiday in honour of Mildred Hubble.' 'Good old Mil!' yelled someone. 'Thanks for the holiday!' And for a moment Jill Murphy is even cheekier, recalling old thrillers: 'Well, well, Agatha,' chuckles Miss Cackle to her villainous sister, 'so we meet again.'

So, yes, we can see that *The Worst Witch* captures exactly the appeal of the school, while at the same time affectionately giggling at it. But this would only explain its success if we knew in the first place why the Chalet School, and books like it, have remained popular for so many generations. It can't be nostalgia, when most readers are far too young to have read the original stories. So why on earth are girls at ordinary day schools fascinated by make-believe private boarding-schools, whose way of life, if it ever did exist, is long dead?

You, the reader, are surely the real expert. Do *you* know the answer?

Stephanie Nettell

Puffin | Modern | Classics

Retail price £5.99 each

See over for details of how to order

P u f f i n | M o d e r n | C l a s s i c s

To order any of the books listed please send a cheque or postal order (payable to Penguin Books Ltd) for the total sum due to:

> **Puffin Modern Classics**
> **PO Box 69**
> **Leighton Buzzard**
> **Bedfordshire**
> **LU7 7ZD**

Please include a list of the title/s and quantity/ies required as well as details of the address that they are to be delivered to.

Alternatively, you may use the credit card hotline for Visa and Mastercard purchases:

> **01525 – 851 945**

Note that a booking charge of fifty pence per order will be made for credit card payments.

Postage and packaging is free for this offer only.

Allow 30 days for delivery (subject to availability of stock).
Offer open to residents of UK only.
This offer is only open until April 1999.

Puffin|Books

For children of all ages, Puffin represents quality and variety – the very best in publishing today around the world.

For complete information about the range of books available from Puffin – and Penguin – please write to:

Dept. EP
Penguin Books Ltd
Bath Road
Harmondsworth
West Drayton
Middlesex
UB7 ODA

Or visit us on the worldwide web at:

www.penguin.com